I AM WHALE MAN

By Jason Blanchard

Cover Artwork Concept:

Susie Blanchard

Finished Cover Artwork:

Caitlin Cash

SO . . .

I'm not sure what the beach looked like that day before we arrived. I've seen photos of the area from before the shrines and the barricades were erected. I can imagine people setting up their beach towels, getting umbrellas from the hotel staff, and playing in the surf. I'm thankful that we showed up early enough that only a few people were out on the beach, and so no one got hurt. I think that would've overshadowed what happened next. For all I know, I might have been charged with manslaughter, because . . . it was my fault we were there in the first place.

I'd lost track of how long I'd been in there.

From the time we left on Wednesday evening, till the time we arrived on Friday morning, it had been about thirty-eight cramped, hot, and smelly hours. Did I mention it was dark and I hadn't seen any light the entire time? At least not until we arrived at the beach. When I finally saw light again, I thought maybe it was "the light." The one you see at the end of the tunnel before God welcomes you home.

It was not.

Most likely if you're reading this book and lived through what happened, then you've seen the amateur phone camera footage. At the time, it was one of the top five online videos, behind a Korean boy band's new music video and fluffy baby ducklings that had accidentally fallen into a grate.

There I was, stumbling out of the mouth of an actual whale onto Miami Beach where I said the prophetic words, "I have a message from God," and became known as the Whale Man.

The whole world changed forever that day.

At the time of writing this book, it's been seven years since that day, and in these seven years, I've never given an interview besides the one on the beach that day.

I haven't spoken publicly about what happened or how I ended up in the whale or why God asked me to be His prophet and say what He wanted me to say, where He wanted me to say it.

I haven't spoken publicly about where I went or what I did afterward.

I especially haven't spoken about what's been going on for the last seven years.

Until now.

It's time.

There are so many places this story could start, and pieces I could or should leave out or gloss over. I can clearly say that I'm not the hero of the story you're about to read. The hero's presence is felt throughout the whole book. There may be moments when you may begin to think I'm actually the villain. I wouldn't even consider myself the main supporting character, because the whale is so much more important to the story than I am, without the whale, this story would be called "I Am Some Guy."

I don't want to waste your time going back too far, to when my parents got divorced, or the day I met my wife, or when we planted the church I pastored.

I do want you to know I have prayed over every sentence I've written and revised. When I pray, I can feel the Holy Spirit say, "Through you, I will write this story, edit this story, promote this story, and get people to read this story. All you need to do is surrender to the process."

So . . . this is me surrendering to the process.

My life goes better when I surrender to God's Will.

It just does.

When I don't, it just doesn't.

I want to take you back to several nights before we, the whale and I, showed up on that beach in Miami.

Back to the night God shook me, and began to burn down everything I had been, so I could become who I've become.

Back to before I was the Whale Man and God's Message caused so much fighting and burning and running and pain.

Back to when He chose me even though He could've chosen someone else; to when He gave me a mission and a message to tell you all, "He's pissed and our time is running out."

—Edgar "Whale Man" White

CHAPTER ONE:
STEP NINE

It was a hot Tuesday night in East Baltimore in late July, and I was attending my weekly Alcoholics Anonymous (AA) meeting at this small church about a mile from my neighborhood. We'd been sitting in our circle listening to each other share how they'd battled alcohol and how alcohol had won before they found AA, and sometimes even after.

When it was my turn in the circle, I stood up and said, "Hi, my name is Eddie and I am an alcoholic," to which everyone replied, in unison, with the customary, "Hi, Eddie."

"And it's been five months since my last drink."

I've been told by the few close friends that've read early versions of this story that I should describe what I look like, for anyone who may have never heard of the Whale Man. So, I am about six-feet tall and, back then, I had black hair and a scruffy beard that I'd been growing to conceal my appearance. I had fifteen tattoos on my arms and chest, most of them were symbols of my Christian faith.

I've been called handsome by my family and also by strangers. I'm an average, typical-looking guy in his mid- to late thirties. I've always had a runner's body, and after I'd quit drinking, my puffy face went away.

Ok . . . back to the AA meeting. I was proud of those five months of sobriety and was happy I was able to make it that far. It felt good to commit to something again and stick with it.

After the meeting, I was hanging out in front of the church with my sponsor, Joal, and he asked if I wanted to get a drink and catch up—and by a drink, we both knew he meant a root beer or coffee.

We headed down to a hole-in-the-wall dive bar that surprisingly had those side-by-side basketball arcade machines. I love that game. It's a game where I can fully concentrate on one thing and compete one-on-one with someone else. We must have played ten games before our forearms locked up and we sat down at a table to talk. For the record, I won eight of those games.

Joal is a solid guy. He's about the same height as me and there have been times when people asked us if we're brothers. We'd say no, but kind of, yes.

He's like a brother to me.

In the beginning of my sobriety, Joal would pick me up and personally take me to every AA meeting, to make sure I got there and didn't back out. He was always there for me in moments of weakness when I chose to call for support. There would be no restoration in my life without Joal's assistance, and I am eternally grateful to God for bringing him into my life.

Thank you, Joal, in case I haven't said it recently.

We sat there talking about life and then Joal asked, "How are you doing on Step Nine?" I hung my head in defeat.

"Gah . . . I'm stuck on Step Nine."

I'd gotten through the first eight steps of the Twelve Steps of AA without much difficulty.

For those of you that don't know what Step Nine is, it is to make amends to the people you hurt during your time of alcoholism. That's all it is, just make amends.

Just. Make. Amends.

I remember sitting there fidgeting with my hands and rubbing the back of my head, which is one of my tells that I'm uncomfortable.

I told Joal I'd made a list, but that when I looked at it, I had no idea where to start. The list seemed overwhelming and there was so much to make amends for.

My list:

- my wife
- my daughter
- Kelley
- the church
- the world
- God

I felt paralyzed.

He told me, "The best way to get started is to get started," which is the same advice I'd give anyone seeking my counsel. But I know that saying and doing are two very different things.

He reminded me, "Making amends means to change the way you acted and the way you thought and to repent from what you had been to the people you hurt."

All of this I knew.

The pit I had dug for myself was so deep and I felt so far down at the bottom of it, I wasn't sure how I was going to get out.

Joal left soon after, but I didn't want to go home and be alone in my apartment, so I sat and stared at my phone like most of the other people were doing in the bar.

I did like many people do when they're afraid to move forward into the unknown—I looked back.

Something something . . . Lot's wife, something something . . . pillar of salt.

I dove into my Instagram account. I hadn't posted anything since the scandal broke, except one brief and sweeping apology. About nine months had passed since everything came to light and I was fired from the church we planted and I pastored.

I stopped posting because I couldn't take any more comments from people. The cruelest comments didn't come from strangers, they came from friends. I know you should never read the comments section, but I did, and I still can't forget them.

I was scrolling through my old photos and stopped on a behind-the-scenes shot from when we took our last family Christmas photo together. We were taking it for the church's annual staff Christmas card we sent to the whole congregation.

My wife looked so beautiful and my daughter's eyes were filled with joy. I looked very dashing in a new suit I'd gotten for the photoshoot. We looked like the perfect family.

All of our faces seemed so happy and I missed that life so much. I would've given anything to go back and tell my younger self, "Eddie, don't mess this up." To tell him there is danger ahead and to be on guard and to protect himself and to protect his family.

But I don't think young-Eddie would've listened. In fact, I know he wouldn't have. He was too proud and arrogant and addicted to the attention to listen.

We hadn't been together as a family since I walked out on them before I got sober. My wife and I only spoke through texts, and mainly to coordinate Thursday night story time for our daughter. Every Thursday night we'd do story time, and it was my favorite and least favorite time of the week because I could hear their voices.

My wife didn't talk directly to me, but I'd hear her say to our daughter, "Are you ready for story time with daddy?" And then when we'd finish, she'd say, "Say goodnight to daddy." And that was it.

Then my daughter would always say, "Goodnight, daddy. When are you coming home?" And my heart would break.

"Soon, baby girl, soon. I'll come home as soon as I can." And I'd hold back my tears until I hung up.

Everything was broken and I had broken it. I wanted to get myself cleaned up before I went home again. I felt like they deserved that. My wife would ask me about once a month when I was coming home, and I'd tell her I'd come home again when I was worthy of her and our daughter's love.

If you would've seen me sitting in the bar alone with tears coming down my face, you may have stopped by and asked if you could pray for me. But no one did.

Sigh.

I kept scrolling and looking at smiles and better days, and

then one photo hit me. It was from when I was on stage as the lead pastor of our church. It was the Sunday I gave the "Missing Children of Heaven" sermon, which would become the one I was most well-known for and why our church attendance and baptisms quickly grew by 300%.

In case you haven't heard of the sermon or didn't get to watch it online before it was removed, it was a sermon about the missing children of Heaven. It was based on how we're all God's children and how He loves us because we are His kids and not because of what we do or don't do, and when we choose to run away from Heaven, we become the missing children of Heaven.

An excerpt from my sermon notes:

To all the runaways in the audience today. There is a "missing child" poster in Heaven with your name and face on it.

Your Heavenly Father misses you so much.

He's not mad. He's not waiting to judge you for where you've been and what you've done, He wants you to come home.

Come home all you runaways.

Come home to a Father that loves you.

Come home all you who are weary and worn out and ready for rest.

Come home to a loving Father waiting with open arms to hug you and kiss your face and whisper gently in your ear, "Welcome home."

It's time.

It's time to come home.

I remember looking out into the audience that day and seeing so many tearful faces of people choosing to return home.

Afterward, we did a whole "Missing Children of Heaven" promotional campaign. The recording of the sermon received more views than any other sermon I'd ever given. It was making an impact. God's runaways were choosing to come home and they were doing it at our church.

Our youth group got the idea to make "Missing Children of Heaven" posters to post around the neighborhood and on social media. We didn't realize how much it would create a stir in people. There were a few people that thought the youth group kids were really missing and started calling the cops to say they'd spotted them near our church.

Regardless, the idea got a lot of attention.

We had to add two extra service times to handle the influx of people. The additional services took a toll on me, because I was preaching more and we needed to manage more staff and volunteers to make everything work.

This is how and when Kelley joined our church staff and we became a part of each other's stories.

Without even thinking about it, I'd brought up Kelley's social media account. She had blocked me, but I could still see her face in her profile pic.

Kelley had, and has, a smile that lights up a room and this overwhelming personality of happiness. She has a carefree beauty that doesn't try too hard.

This part of the book is difficult because my daughter will read this and, although we've done a good job over the last seven years letting her know that mommy and I went through a difficult time, she still doesn't know why.

So, sweetheart, I'm sorry for what you're about to read.

Your mommy and I will sit down with you before this book comes out, and we'll explain everything to you ourselves.

My wife already knows this part of the story quite well. We've spent a long time in counseling and I've answered all the questions she's wanted to know. I've given her "100%" of what happened. So, none of this will be a shock to her, but it may be unknown to you.

The press and numerous unauthorized documentaries did a lot of digging and reporting on the scandal, so it's possible you already know what happened. But now you'll hear it from my perspective.

I'm not trying to justify my actions; I'm hoping to provide clarity on things that have been misexplained by people who weren't directly involved in what happened.

But I get that when someone says they're not trying to justify their actions, they're normally trying to justify their actions.

I was unfaithful to my wife with Kelley and it was one of the reasons I was fired from my role as the lead pastor of the church we planted years ago on the outskirts of Washington, D.C.

Kelley has read everything you're about to read and has given her blessing and permission for it to be published. She did request for a few revisions to be made, but it doesn't change how and what happened. She mainly cleared up a few things that I was a little fuzzy on because of the alcohol.

Kelley and I, and most of our leadership team, were traveling out of state on a work trip and for off-site team-building adventures. We were visiting another church we helped plant. My wife was supposed to come with us, but our daughter wasn't feeling well so she stayed home with her.

I wish I would've made a lot of different decisions that night when I was pacing outside of Kelley's hotel room. I must have paced outside her door for five minutes before I stopped and knocked and waited. My heart was racing faster than it had ever before. Looking back, it didn't even feel like I was making the decision, I was acting on my urges.

My wife and I had a good marriage and I loved her very much, but I hadn't felt this kind of desire and excitement in a long time.

Kelley was intoxicating and I was drunk on her.

She answered the door with a smile that I can still recall to this day and I asked if I could come in to talk. She welcomed me in, and I broke my vows to my wife.

That night set off a chain reaction of decisions and consequences that led me to sitting alone, crying in that bar.

As you can see, this is why I wasn't looking forward to Step Nine—I had a lot to make amends for and I didn't know where to start. I left the bar that night sad and depressed and feeling like the mountain in my path was too high to climb.

As I walked the mile through the city streets back to my apartment, I passed an open liquor store and paused in front of it for a moment. I don't know if it was the depressing trip down memory lane or the daunting task of making amends, but in that moment, I felt an overwhelming urge to drink.

I paced back and forth for a few minutes, debating whether to go in and hoping for the feeling to fade. As the urges began to pass, I decided to keep walking toward my apartment . . . until I quickly changed my mind and walked back and in through the door.

Yes, I also see a pattern of behavior here.

My hand was shaking, and I could feel that rush of searching for a comforting bottle of bourbon. They had a surprisingly good selection. I found one of my old favorites and headed to the register to pay for it.

The man behind the counter grinned at me and asked, "Will this be all?" I nodded, yes. Then he paused and said, "You look familiar, have I seen you in here before?" *Great.* This guy may have gone to my old church or had seen the scandal on the news and I no longer felt anonymous. I had moved an hour away hoping to escape my past, but now I thought I hadn't gone far enough. I grimaced back at him and said, "Don't think so, but I've been told I have one of those faces."

He continued to study my face trying to picture where he knew me from, "Are you sure we haven't met before, you look so familiar?"

I told him I had recently moved to the area and this was my first time in and, again, "I get this a lot." He didn't seem convinced as he started to ring me up.

Then he stopped suddenly as if he finally figured out where he knew me from and looked me right in the eyes, but this time, he seemed different.

"God has a message He wants you to deliver for Him."

At this point, I was annoyed and quickly replied, "Look, I

don't know who you think I am, but your joke sucks and I'm about to leave."

He kept staring right as me as he continued. "He wants you to go to Miami Beach and proclaim these exact words, "'God is going to cleanse our world with fire in forty days.'"

At this point I was pissed and was pretty sure this guy was messing with me. "Look, I don't know who you think I am, but *ha ha ha*, jokes on me."

But then he said, "To know what I have said is true you won't be able to speak again until you find the fox in the hen house."

I wanted to reply, but no words came out. I was speechless —meaning, I was literally unable to speak . . . at all. I kept trying, because, trust me, I had a lot to still say to this guy, but there was nothing.

As you might imagine, I was confused and frustrated, so I quickly left the liquor store, without the bourbon, and started heading back to my apartment.

I tried everything to get words out.

Yelling.

Whispering.

I was mute.

I could think of words, but I couldn't say them.

That was about the time I spotted my first "signs," as I like to call them. They started that night and still continue to this day.

I saw a business storefront that had windows painted with giant letters, "FIRE SALE! EVERYTHING MUST GO!" And then a city bus passed by that had an oversized "VISIT MIAMI BEACH" billboard on the side of it.

As I continued to make my way to my apartment, I passed by another neighborhood dive bar and a pretty girl standing outside yelled, "FIREBALL," in my face, and, "free shots of Fireball inside."

I wanted to say, "gross," but when I tried, there was nothing.

As a side note, I believe Fireball was created by the Devil in the pits of Hell.

I said it.

Fight me.

I could go on and on about all the "signs" I started to see everywhere.

Like this next one . . .

I was about to cross the street at the light next to my apartment when I noticed a street preacher had set up a mobile church and was yelling into a megaphone.

I wasn't a fan of street preachers, especially on a Tuesday night when people are out trying to have a good time. Street preaching to me has always felt like some self-righteous jerk trying to get attention for himself by making other people feel bad about their lives. I've changed my thoughts on street preaching since then, but on that night, I rolled my eyes as I listened to this guy telling people they were going to Hell if they didn't repent of their ways.

Who wants to be called a sinner while they're trying to get a couple drinks and pick up a random stranger from a bar to take home for the night?

Look, I know that's kind of what I did when I was a pastor, but I was on a stage and people chose to show up for it.

I always felt street preachers drove people away from attending church.

He was talking so loud that his crappy speakers couldn't take it and all I could hear was crackly distortions and feedback. Overall, he had very low-budget production quality.

While I was waiting for the pedestrian light to change, he made eye contact with me.

Great.

"You there, prophet of God," he said with his finger pointing right at me. "Why are you running from God and His calling on your life?"

I really wanted that light to change.

"You can't run from God," he said pointing up toward the sky, and then he repeated it, but this time much louder, "YOU CAN'T RUN FROM GOD!"

Let's just say, that's not the last time I would hear that.

It's a bit of a recurring theme.

The light finally changed and I quickly crossed and headed toward my apartment. I could still hear him yelling in the distance. "GOD IS GOING TO BRING DOWN FIRE FROM HEAVEN AND YOU'LL SEE, YOU'LL ALL SEE YOUR WICKEDNESS!"

I finally made it inside my apartment, thankfully, without another supernatural incident.

My apartment was like one of those "middle-aged-man-ruined-his-life" starter packs. There was a single mattress on the floor, a lone lamp to light the whole room, and two boxes for laundry: one box for dirty clothes and one for clean clothes.

Sundays were my laundromat days.

My collection of empty pizza boxes and to-go containers created a special kind of potpourri for the place. I called it "desperate man who cheated on his wife and chose to live in solitary confinement."

If there isn't a candle that smells like that already, there should be.

It'd be a big hit.

Once I finally had a few moments to sit and think about what happened at the liquor store, I thought about how God didn't do things like this anymore. I'd studied the Bible and preached sermons and I'd heard the stories of prophets and God calling people to speak on His behalf, but that all happened a long time ago.

I didn't think that kind of thing would happen again.

Especially to me.

Maybe I'd gone crazy . . . and given myself muteness due to extreme guilt over the decisions I'd made.

That seemed more rational than the actual God of the Bible telling me to go to Miami Beach to say that He will cleanse the world with fire in forty days.

But, since there's a video of me on a beach in Miami saying those words, we all can see what's coming.

As I sat down on my mattress and reached for my cellphone charging cable, so I could do my before-bed-scrolling, I accidentally knocked over my large stack of books. They were books on leadership, God's grace, and memoirs of people I admired.

And . . . my Bible.

All the other books I'd stacked on top of it had fallen over, exposing it. It'd been a while since I'd looked through it or even wanted to open it.

I picked it up and flipped through its pages. I'd forgotten how many personal messages were written along the margins. Not, like, notes I had written, but notes people had written to me and to my wife.

Before we left the church we previously attended, to plant a new one, my wife passed our Bible around to the youth group, friends that had been in our small groups, and many of our closest friends, and they all wrote in it like a high school yearbook.

There were notes of sincere encouragement and genuine gratitude and stories of how my wife and I had helped them through difficult times.

It was clear to see that we had made an impact . . . together.

Until I messed everything up.

Heavy sigh.

Before I closed it and then scrolled through my phone until I fell asleep, I took the sheet of paper I'd written my "Step Nine" list on and stuck it inside.

That would need to be a future-me problem, because current-me had enough problems of his own.

CHAPTER TWO: BURN IT DOWN

The fox in the hen house.

Miami Beach.

Fire.

As you might imagine there was much on my mind as I got dressed and ready for work the next morning. I kept trying to talk but nothing came out.

It was still a thing.

During my commute to the office, I came to the conclusion that I was either losing my mind, stuck in one of those dreams within a dream, or that The God of the Universe wanted me to take a trip to Miami Beach.

Everywhere I turned there were more "signs," just like the night before.

Bumper stickers.

Billboards.

The morning show on the radio talked about how forest fires were burning out of control in the West, and, "Coming up next, we've got a chance for the seventh caller to win an all-expenses-paid vacation to Miami Beach."

Maybe I should've called in.

At the same time, a fire truck—with lights spinning and sirens blaring—passed on the other side of the beltway heading in the direction I was coming from.

Either God was trying to keep my attention, or I had a serious case of cognitive bias going on and was seeing and hearing things I wanted to see and hear.

It's like when you buy a white car and all you see are white cars everywhere.

I saw God . . . everywhere.

When I pulled into the parking lot of the building where I worked, I did my ritualistic heavy sigh, followed by a ten-minute meditation exercise, and then a final heavy sigh before I walked from my assigned parking spot up the five flights of stairs to my assigned cubicle.

I worked as an inside salesman at a septic tank company.

My job was to sell septic tanks to housing developers.

Septic tanks.

Soon after I'd gotten sober, I took steps to put my life back together and to provide for my wife and daughter. I didn't want to be a deadbeat dad and I had hopes that my wife and I could eventually reconcile.

So, I looked for work.

After searching and applying to countless places, the septic tank company was the first one willing to hire me after the scandal and all the scathing articles attacking my integrity and character.

Honestly, I struggled to apply anywhere at all because I

didn't know what I was capable of doing or what I wanted to do. I'd been in professional ministry since college, and I was unsure if those skills would transfer to any other career.

There was nothing that interested me like leading a church and preaching on stage. I wanted an audience, a sound system and lights, authority, purpose, but instead . . . I sold septic tanks.

When I interviewed for the job, they searched for me online like all the other companies had, but my supervisor, Steven, thought that my despair and lack of options would drive me to be a hard worker. During the interview, he said, "If you could sell Jesus to people, you can probably sell septic tanks to people."

That's always stuck with me.

Within a few minutes of sitting down at my desk, Roger, a coworker of mine, popped his head into my cubicle to ask, "What'd you do last night?"

Roger was my only friend at work because once my other coworkers searched online for my name and saw that I was a former pastor who cheated on his wife, they decided I wasn't someone they wanted to get to know.

No one actually ever told me that, but it was the assumption I'd made for why no one ever talked to me.

Maybe they were worried I'd sit down and tell them about my Lord and Savior, Jesus Christ, while they were trying to sell septic tanks.

I doubt I would've done that if given the chance.

Roger didn't care about that stuff and I really appreciated that about him. I could tell he wanted a friend, as much as

I wanted a friend. He did have this habit of striking up a conversation with a question, so that I'd ask him the same question, so he'd tell me really salacious things about himself. So, I knew when he was asking me about what I'd done the night before, what he really wanted was to tell me what he'd done the night before.

Roger was an above-average attractive guy. He was a few inches taller than me, took care of himself, and dressed well. He had style. Essentially, everything in his life was designed for him to get a woman back to his condo for the night, but only one night.

Since I wasn't able to talk, I held up a post-it note: LOST VOICE. CAN'T TALK.

Roger seemed confused by the fact I couldn't talk, but only paused for a second before telling me about the drinks he had the night before. Roger kept track of his alcoholic beverages, the amounts, the order of consumption, and how buzzed he was at any given time before he shared a story. It was like he was building context for what happened next. "I started with two shots of Fireball," he said as he glanced around the office. It was like he was always letting me in on a secret. Then he told me about the two Coronas, three Jagerbombs, and he finished off the night with a Jack and Coke before taking home a random girl he'd met at the bar.

To me, Roger drank crappy liquor.

I always listened to Roger's stories because I genuinely liked him. I could see a lot of myself in him and how he lived his life. Underneath his stories of competitive drinking and sexual conquests, I felt like he was sad, searching for love, and desperate for acceptance.

Maybe I was projecting.

Before he left my cubicle, he told me that Steven wanted to have an all-hands sales meeting and a working lunch starting at 11 am. Then he said, "it's going to suck that you can't talk, Steven sent an email at 5:15 this morning and he seems really fired up."

Steven had been out of the office since Friday at a sales conference. He said it was a conference run by sales people, with talks from sales people, for sales people who want to increase their sales and reach their maximum sales potential. He suggested for all of us to go . . . I declined his invitation.

Who knows, if I had gone, I might have missed God's mandatory volunteer opportunity to be his whale-bound messenger.

Most of my morning was wasted looking at social media apps, checking and replying to work emails, and looking up "Can mental health disorders cause muteness?"—which it can, in some circumstances. After going down one heck of a rabbit hole of mental illness diagnoses, it seemed like I didn't meet the criteria for any of those types of disorders.

I killed enough of my morning doing nothing, that it was time for our sales meeting with Steven in the conference room, where I took my assigned seat by the window.

Sometimes I fantasized about jumping through the glass and plummeting to the ground below. It seemed like a better alternative than sitting through another exhilarating meeting about selling septic tanks.

There were six of us on the sales team. Roger, myself, and a few others. I sincerely can't remember any of their names or what they looked like.

Steven was at the front of the conference room with one of those three-legged easels propping up a huge pad of paper. It was the kind of paper that you could pull off, in giant sheets, and stick to the wall. On the left side of the paper, he wrote these letters, like this:

F

I

R

E

I let out a heavy sigh.

Steven was a real salesman. Like, a *real*-real salesman. He read books on sales, listened to podcasts and webinars on sales, and was fearless when selling. I don't know for sure, but I'm guessing he could quote every line from the classic movie about salesmen, *Glengarry Glen Ross*. He was an "always be closing" kind of guy.

He was average looking, a little taller than me. Steven enjoyed talking about how being a salesman made his life better. He talked about his better car, better house, and better wife.

I could tell he was a little more fired up than normal, because his hand was shaking from what was most likely his third energy drink of the morning.

He took a moment to pause and compose himself before he looked at all of us and said, "10x." And I thought to myself, *here we go.* He reminded me of how I looked when I took the stage—focused, determined, ready to inspire and change lives.

I was concerned, very concerned.

Steven stared each one of us in the eye for what felt like an eternity, before he pointed to the oversized pad of paper and rhetorically asked, "What does the F stand for?" Before any of us could answer his question, he boldly proclaimed, "It stands for fierce."

He passionately wrote his answer on the easel.

F = Fierce

I

R

E

One down.

Steven wasn't and isn't a bad guy, and I was thankful for the job. He gave me a chance when no one else would. I'm truly sorry I couldn't get excited about selling septic tanks like he could. He was so confident he could sell anything and I believe, if given the opportunity, he could even sell Jesus to people.

"You're a competent and capable sales team so why are the sales numbers from the last quarter so abysmal at best, terrible at worst," he said with a little wavering in his voice, which was most likely from the energy drinks. "We need to be fierce on the phone, fierce in our emails, and fierce in the way we wine and dine these developers. We need to close. There are no more excuses."

It was like a salesman's version of a Come to Jesus sermon.

"Fierce!"

If he had a podium, he would've pounded his fists down upon it.

Then he pointed to the "I" on the easel and looked directly at me. "Eddie, what does 'I' stand for?" I could've sworn it was another rhetorical question that he would eventually answer himself, but he didn't, so we kept staring at each other waiting for the other to respond. It was awkward for all of us. We just kept staring at one another, so I held up my post-it note: LOST VOICE. CAN'T TALK.

Steven's face twitched a little and, without skipping a beat, he said, "Well then you're even more useless to me than you were before."

That hurt.

Suddenly and thankfully . . . we were all saved by a bell. The automatic fire alarm began blaring throughout the office. Someone stuck their head into the conference room and said, "There's a lot of smoke coming from the break room."

We quickly evacuated the building and watched as it went up in flames.

The fire department arrived promptly and fought the flames back, but it was a total loss. I'm glad I always travel everywhere with my backpack. It had all my personal things inside of it. I had everything with me I needed, so there was nothing at my assigned cubicle I was going to miss.

I looked around at all my coworkers, especially Roger and Steven, standing around trying to figure out their next steps. I couldn't help but grin. Steven looked over my way as I held up a new post-it note I'd written him.

I = I Quit

Felt good.

You may have seen documentaries and articles over the

years that suggested I burned down the office by starting a fire in the break room before the meeting. The septic tank company was the only place willing to give me a chance at that time in my life, so . . . no, I didn't burn it down.

It has also been suggested by those same documentaries and articles, that I also burned down my own apartment on the same day.

Wait, . . . What?

Remember that fire truck I passed on the way to work that morning? It had been heading to my apartment.

After I quit my job, I drove back to my apartment to find it completely burned down and still smoldering. An arson investigator was on the scene taking notes for his report as I walked up and I think he could tell by the shocked look on my face that it was my apartment, but he still asked, "Is this your place?"

I nodded yes.

He got so excited to see me. His face had this big amazed smile on it as he reached into the bag he was carrying and pulled out a sealed evidence bag with my Bible inside. The same Bible with all the personalized messages written in it. He removed it from the plastic bag, held it out to me, and said, "The whole place is a total loss, except for this."

He was right, it was in perfect condition.

"It's a miracle," he said, handing it to me. "I found it sitting in the charred remains of all your possessions." He started to pull his phone out of his pocket. "Mind if I take a photo of you with it?"

I shook my head no.

I could tell he was disappointed. But there weren't enough post-it notes in my backpack to explain the many reasons why I didn't want to end up on the internet again, especially for a "Miracle Bible."

He handed me his business card. "Well, if you change your mind, I'd love to share this story with others." I nodded yes as I stuck the Bible and his card in my backpack.

Looking back on it, I should've let him take the photos. It might've helped my credibility after I got spit out of the whale a couple days later.

Probably not.

He said a lot of other stuff about the fire and about his report and asked if I needed anything. I wasn't really paying much attention. My mind was other places.

My work and my apartment had burned down, and I still couldn't speak.

My life was less than ideal.

I walked back to where I'd parked my car along the street, plopped down into the driver's seat, and reclined it all the way back so I could meditate. I needed to clear my mind and settle myself.

My rule for meditation was and still is, do it when I don't feel like it, because I know that's when I need it the most.

I laid there hoping for a sign of what to do next. I thought about going home to my family, but I wasn't ready. I thought about going to my parent's house and asking to stay with them, but I didn't want to do that again. I thought about texting Joal for help and seeing if he knew of a place to stay or any place hiring, but I felt tired of bothering him with my problems. And if I'm being absolutely vulnerable with you here, I had intrusive thoughts about ending it all.

I didn't know what to do.

It was the closest I'd come to praying in a long time.

As I was sitting there with my eyes closed, deep in self-guided meditation, contemplating my next steps, I heard someone messing with the windshield wipers on my car.

I quickly opened my eyes and raised my seat and couldn't believe what I saw. There was a flyer for the grand opening of the Hen House Chicken and Fish restaurant stuck to my windshield. It was a brand-new restaurant that had recently opened not too far from my neighborhood.

The hen house.

The fox?!?

I GPS'd the address and the Hen House was only a fifteen-minute hike away. I grabbed my backpack and the flyer, and started walking. As I got closer, I kept thinking, *How dare God burn down my stuff?* I thought about getting fired from the church, how things ended with Kelley, my wife's disappointment, my daughter's sadness, and everything else in my life that'd been taken from me.

How dare God?

I'd spent years building His Kingdom and this was my reward?

The Hen House's red neon sign taunted me as I got closer and closer. I was so focused on it I didn't notice the homeless man sitting by the entrance until he yelled at me, "You can't run from God!"

It stopped me in my tracks.

He stared at me and yelled again, "You can't run from God!" I looked down at him sitting there, holding onto his handmade sign asking for change, and I held up my index finger, to express to him, "Hold that thought, I'll be right back."

I flung the door open and walked right into the Hen House Chicken and Fish; standing right there behind the register was this tall teenager, with a name tag that said, "FOX." He smiled at me and said, "Welcome to Hen House Chicken and Fish, what would you like today?" I opened my mouth to speak and the words fell out, "Not this."

The chicken was good.

Not great.

But . . . I could talk again.

I could whisper again.

I could yell again.

So . . . 4/5 stars, would visit again.

As I left the Hen House with my voice back and a tender drumstick in my hand, the same homeless man yelled at me, "You can't run from God," to which I replied, "Yes, I absolutely can!"

I'm not exactly proud of what happened next.

At the time, I was so angry with God; I thought if this homeless man was a conduit for God to deliver a message to me, then maybe he'd be a conduit for me to deliver a message to God.

"Yes, I can run from You," I said, or at least that's how I remember launching into my rant. "How dare You! I'm not some hand puppet you can make do and say whatever You want," I said, as my voice got louder. There were a lot of other things I said, but it's all kind of a blur of swearing and hand gestures. I do remember ending my self-righteous public outburst with, "I'm taking my free will and doing whatever I want with it and You can't stop me."

The homeless man looked stunned. As if he had no idea what I was talking about. I quickly began to question my own sanity and if God had sent this man to deliver a message at all, until he calmly replied, "You can't run from God, Eddie."

Imagine my surprise.

There was so much else I wanted to tell God, but all I could say was, "I'm done."

It was like I was taking my ball and going home. I was that kind of kid growing up. Whenever something didn't go my way when I was playing with the neighborhood kids, I'd pack my toys, video games, or sports equipment and walk home.

"Get someone else to be Your puppet," I mumbled as I turned to walk away.

"Eddie! You can't run from God!" the homeless man yelled as he stood up to follow me. He kept yelling the same thing, over and over, as he pursued me down the street. Then, another homeless person joined him, then another, then another, all yelling the same thing. But not all together like a chorus, more like a jumbled mess of, "You can't run from God!"

That's when I started to actually run.

When I've shared this story with close personal friends, they've asked if this was, like, a "hoard" of homeless people? And the answer is, yes.

A hoard of homeless people was running after me.

What happened next is actually provable—there are weather reports of a meteorological mystery that came out of nowhere. It happened at the exact time and in the exact location I was in.

The sky quickly turned black and there was lightning all around us. It was like a disaster movie. The only thing missing was the ominous fog. The rain came down so hard it felt like hail. Maybe it was.

It felt like nowhere was safe.

That's about the time I had made it all the way to the Hanover Street Bridge. My neighborhood wasn't far from South Baltimore and the river that feeds into the Chesapeake Bay. The Hanover Street Bridge is one of the longer bridges in downtown Baltimore. It has four lanes with nice walking paths on either side. It's right next to one of my favorite places in the city to get steamed crabs.

I made it about half way across the bridge, with the heavy rain and lightning, when I saw another hoard of homeless people coming at me from the opposite direction.

Imagine my surprise.

With the storm on top of me and hoards in front and behind me, I felt trapped.

I was angry.

I was wet.

I was scared.

I was done.

I stood there at the edge of the bridge looking down at the

water below and I couldn't imagine another way out.

I let out a primal scream. "WHHHHHHHHHHYYYYYYYY-YYYYYYYY?!?!?!"

That scream had been buried deep inside of me for months, maybe years. All this pain, all this hurt, all this frustration, all this doubt, all this led to me yelling at God, "Why me?"

What happened next was so unexpected, I clearly heard a whisper in the storm, "So a beautiful story of redemption and love could be told."

This whisper wasn't like anything I'd ever heard before.

It felt like, for the first time in my life, God had spoken to me.

A wave of peace flooded my mind, body, and spirit.

So, I jumped off the bridge.

The water was colder than I expected and I sank faster than I anticipated.

And then . . . I was swallowed by the whale.

CHAPTER THREE: SO MUCH TRUTH

Let me assure you, the first thoughts you have when you're swallowed by a great fish are not that God is doing Jonah again.

It's literally the one thought that doesn't come to mind.

I only preached on the Bible's account of Jonah once during my time as a pastor and I'll be honest, I struggled with the accuracy of the story. If it wasn't for Jesus mentioning that Jonah spent three days in the great fish, I would've discounted the entire story as a metaphor or an analogy.

Imagine my surprise when I found myself in an actual whale.

"What was it like in there?" is the question I get asked most.

It was dark, wet, and smelled like leftover sushi.

I didn't like it.

It was uncomfortable and confining.

To this day, I have a recurring nightmare: I'm back in the whale, I feel like I'm suffocating, it surfaces for air, and I can breathe again.

Repeat.

Over and over.

I was never in the "belly" of the whale. I was in the mouth. And there was enough room to stretch out my arms and legs. But I mainly stayed in the fetal position the whole time. The whale's tongue moved if I moved, so I tried to stay still. My goal was to keep the whale happy so I wouldn't be eaten or spit out.

When I was "swallowed," the whale's mouth was still full of water and I bounced around chaotically inside, slowly drowning, until it either swallowed the water or blew it out its blowhole. Either way, I could finally breathe again. The pressure inside kept changing, like an airplane constantly taking off and landing. I think my ear drums are still a little damaged to this day. At least that's what I tell my wife and daughter when they ask me for something from across the house and I can't figure out what they've said.

"What? Sorry, can't hear so well, I was in a whale this one time."

I did check my phone once to see if it had a signal. It had stopped working when I hit the water.

That was unfortunate.

The whale's heartbeat was oddly soothing. *Dum dum, dum dum, dum dum . . .* so soothing.

If you're still unclear what it was like in there, then take a small mouse and put it in your mouth. You and the mouse will most likely survive the experience, but neither of you will enjoy it.

"How were you able to breathe?"

It was a miracle.

"How did you make it so quickly to Miami Beach?"

Another miracle.

"What did you do in the whale?"

Nothing much.

Which was kind of the point of the whale. For the first time in a very long time, I couldn't go anywhere or do anything and God had my undivided attention.

The overall experience was terrible. Until it wasn't.

Once the newness and shock wore off and I believed I was actually still alive and not in some weird whale-mouth purgatory, the thought finally crossed my mind that God might be doing Jonah again.

I remember quietly saying aloud, "God, why am I here?"

God whispered to my heart, "Eddie, why are you here?"

Ugh. Don't you hate it when you ask a question and get a question in response?

It's taken me years of therapy, prayer, and self-reflection to understand the answer to that question. I've learned that God doesn't answer questions with questions because He doesn't know the answers. He asks questions so we can find the answers buried within ourselves.

In the darkness of the whale, a lifetime of harshly lit memories overwhelmed me like a flood.

First, the memories came like flashes.

Flashes of when I stole packs of baseball cards and pieces of candy from the convenience store by our apartment when I was seven. My mom eventually caught me when I couldn't explain how I had so many cards and a never-ending supply of candy. My father made me go back to apologize and return everything I'd taken.

They banned me for life.

Flashes of when I was twelve and my friends and I found an old cardboard box of weathered hard-core porn magazines in the woods. We all sat on this old dirty couch that was there and looked through the pictures as we giggled. I took one of the magazines with me and hid it under my mattress and spent many nights searing those photos into my brain.

This began a lifetime struggle with pornography.

Flashes of when I was nine and my mom and dad said they weren't going to be married anymore and how it was for the best for everyone. Which turned into flashes of new schools, new friends, new apartments, and new problems.

It wasn't best for anyone.

I saw flashes of my first kiss, my first time on stage, my first heartbreak.

They didn't relent.

I saw when my daughter was born and I saw her face for the first time and she yawned and my heart melted.

I saw when we got the keys from the realtor to the community playhouse we leased to convert into the church and how happy we were seeing our dreams become a reality.

I saw the excessive empty bottles of wine in the recycling bin when I'd take it out on Thursday mornings and how I thought about cutting back every time I saw it but never did.

So many flashes, so many memories, so much sadness and joy, heartbreak and rejoicing, and sins and forgiveness.

The worst part of being in the whale wasn't being in the whale, it was being all alone with my thoughts and my past decisions.

Even now, after years of therapy, there are times the flashes come, the flooding of memories, and it can still be too much.

I consider the flashes of memories a blessing compared to the memories that lingered. The lingering memories were like being a spectator on the sidelines of my past-self, which I call past-me.

The first lingering memory was the Christmas card photo-shoot and I could see it all, feel it all, and was helpless as I watched past-me, and my past-wife and past-daughter all together, laughing and enjoying life . . . until past-me took out his phone. That's when I could see my wife's expression change from happiness to disappointment and my daughter's eyes quickly turned from joy to sadness.

There was past-me, scrolling through his feed, responding to stranger's messages, and seeing how many likes his posts had gotten. He was ever-present, but always-unavailable to the people closest to him. Past-me had become addicted to attention and no matter how much he got, it was never enough.

In the before times, my wife and I met in college at an off-campus house party. She was a friend of a friend, and when we were introduced, I was instantly attracted to her, which sent me into a strange mode of peacocking where I tried to be the funniest guy in the room. She was less than impressed, and I think that made me want to try even harder to win her over.

I found her on social media after the party and slid into her

DMs, where she found me equally annoying and told me to stop trying to impress her, and to be myself. So, I did, and she liked it. We started dating, fell in love, and got married.

We did all the normal married things: got an apartment, finished school, got jobs, and found a local church to attend together. They had this great youth group and my wife and I got heavily involved and loved it. After some time, the church leadership asked if I would like to speak about my own faith, on stage in front of the kids, and I killed it, and was instantly hooked on preaching.

It felt like a calling.

When my wife and I weren't working at our day jobs, we were at the church, spending time with the youth, and they became like a huge extended family.

I grew up an only child from a broken home.

Family is what I'd been looking for my whole life.

I'd finally found it, so of course I wanted more of it.

One day, my wife and I were out for a hike and I told her I wanted the both of us to start a church together. She said, "yes," much faster than when I had asked her to marry me.

We found a church planting organization, we applied, and we went through all the stages of approval, training, counseling, and coaching.

They helped us put together a great launch team of many of the youth group kids that had been with us through the years and were now in college and looking for a cause to support.

We found a great location on the outskirts of Washington, D.C. The location was selected because we felt called to reach a community of influential people that we hoped to influence for the Gospel. The congregation quickly became made up of young professionals from politics, media outlets, and activist organizations dedicated to social change.

Soon after the church doors opened, my wife became pregnant with our one and only daughter. We hadn't been trying, but we weren't *not* trying either, and we both felt like it was a blessing.

My wife decided to stay at home with our daughter, and although I supported it, I missed her daily presence around the church. She took care of a lot of the tasks needed for the church that could be done at home when our daughter was napping or sleeping at night.

The Lord blessed the church and it grew quickly.

We preached and lived out the hope, forgiveness, and grace of the Gospel. We took care of the needs of our community and fed the homeless. We loved one another like Christ loved the Church.

Then, a website that focuses on how preachers dress, voted me one of the ten sexiest preachers in America.

It was unwanted attention.

At first.

My social media following blew up.

So, I told myself I could use the attention to reach more people for the Gospel because of a bigger personal platform.

Lies.

Deep down, I knew the Christmas card photo shoot wasn't for my family or for the church, it was for me and my online followers. That's why my wife's expression changed and my daughter's eyes became sad when I reached for my phone, because they'd watched for years from the front row as I became an "influencer."

Past-me was completely oblivious.

Like I said before, the flashes of memories were a blessing compared to the ones that lingered like this.

Being in the whale was an emotional roller coaster that I wanted to get off, but I was strapped in, and no matter what, I was going where it was taking me.

The next lingering memory transported me to the morning of my most popular sermon . . . "The Missing Children of Heaven."

I watched while past-me stood in his walk-in closet picking the right shirt to go with the right pants, then changing his shirt, and then changing his pants. Past-me tried on four pairs of his twenty-two pairs of designer sneakers, to find the right ones to convey the message of, "God's desire for his missing children to come home."

Heavy sigh.

I spent more time that morning picking an outfit than I did praying for the message I was about to preach.

Once past-me did finally get to the church that morning and the rehearsals wrapped, I watched as he scolded the tech team volunteers. Past-me was frustrated that he couldn't hear himself properly in the monitors. So, he yelled, "it's like a freaking clown show in here today. People come here to hear me preach and if I can't hear myself preaching, then how will I know if I'm making an impact for the Kingdom."

This wasn't the first time or the last time I yelled at volunteers. I wanted every church service to be perfect so that people would think I was perfect, and if people thought I was perfect, they'd follow me and I'd lead them to God.

I was a toxic shepherd.

About an hour after that outburst, past-me was on stage, smiling and preaching, and telling God's children, "It's time to come home."

Afterward, past-me waited in the lobby as tear-stained faces came up to thank him and praise him for his preaching abilities. They mentioned how God spoke to their hearts and how they couldn't wait to tell others about the blessing the church had become for them.

What past-me heard was how he, Eddie the humble pastor, spoke to them and how they couldn't wait to tell others about the blessing he, Eddie the humble pastor, had become for them.

Trust me.

I know.

After that Sunday, church attendance tripled, more service times were added, new full-time staff members were hired, and past-me wasn't equipped to handle what happened next.

Trust me.

I know.

The next lingering memory was . . . past-me pacing back and forth in front of Kelley's hotel room door.

At this moment, past-me still had a choice to make. It was a choice he'd made and hadn't made a thousand times in his mind.

Watching him pace back and forth was like watching righteousness and sin fighting it out to see which one would win.

It wasn't until past-me knocked and past-Kelley opened the door and past-me asked to go in and past-Kelley said yes, that we passed the point of no return.

No matter how much I yelled at past-them to choose differently, it was no use, the past *was*, and I could only helplessly spectate.

Righteousness lost that round.

If only I could say things began innocently.

Kelley was hired to help with scheduling singers and musicians for our worship team. The church had become well-known for our worship music and excellence was the expectation for each and every service. We didn't have full-time musicians on staff so we had to source them every single week, which became difficult as we increased the number of services. We now needed them on Saturday nights, too, and for a longer time on Sunday mornings. Not to mention we were competing with other churches in the area for the top talent.

She excelled at her job and was very easy to work with. We bonded over our love of music and performing. We had both done theater in high school and college, and we could talk for hours about anything and everything.

We both did what we could to keep professional and spiritual guardrails in place. We never met alone in an office with the door closed or went anywhere where it was only the two of us. But, one day the whole leadership team was supposed to hang out after work and Kelley and I were the only ones that showed up.

We told ourselves, "We're coworkers. It isn't an issue." We spent the next couple of hours drinking beers and sharing stories. Looking back on it, it was a date. Not like a *date*-date, but it had all the characteristics of a date. It wasn't the last time we ended up hanging out alone together.

I quickly looked forward to having nights like that.

Look, I knew it was wrong when I didn't want to tell my wife where I had been or who I had been with. I told her I was doing church things with church people. I would tell her, "I was doing my job."

Lies.

Kelley and I never set out to have an affair.

My wife was supposed to go with us on that trip when it happened. Once she couldn't come with us, I became consumed with the idea of being intimate with Kelley while we were both away.

The first night of the trip, the whole team went out for dinner and drinks, and past-me drank a little extra to help with the anxiety and feelings he felt. The whole team had a great time laughing and sharing stories and headed back to the hotel to turn in for the night. Past-me went straight to his room after saying goodnight to everyone. He sat on the bed and did everything he could to not leave the room. He texted his wife, "I love you, turning in for the night." She texted back and asked if he wanted to talk with her and their daughter, but past-me replied, "It's late, been a long day, and I'm turning in for the night, talk in the morning. Love you!"

That should've been the end of the night.

But past-me texted past-Kelley, "You still up?"

"Yes."

So past-me . . . I . . . got up and walked to her room.

Knocking.

Invitations.

It was gut wrenching to watch past-me and past-Kelley be intimate. I had always imagined the "memories" of our time together would be treasured keepsakes, but they aren't, not even close.

It wasn't the only time we were intimate during the trip.

The next morning, we did what we could to hide our glances and flirtations from the rest of the team. I slipped her my room key while we were all gathering for breakfast, right before I gave the morning prayer.

Then we returned home.

The fantasy was over.

Reality smacked me hard.

When Kelley and I were on the trip, we talked about it being an isolated incident, not something that we would keep doing. That plan didn't last long after we returned home.

The shame cycle is powerful.

We felt so much shame for what we'd done, that we'd distract ourselves by being intimate, and then we'd feel bad about it, that we'd distract ourselves again by being intimate. The whole experience felt like a repetitive form of intoxicated death.

Repeat.

Over and over.

Until, we got caught.

My wife found texts, then emails, and then found us together by surprising us at the church, in my office. I can still see the look on her face if I close my eyes. She shined a great big light on what I was hoping to keep in the shadows.

This was about two months after the trip.

After a week of my wife's sobbing and silence, she spoke.

My wife told me to end it and to get professional help.

I told her I would and I would.

But I didn't and I didn't.

Kelley and I continued seeing each other for a few more weeks.

Shame cycle.

It wasn't until my wife confided in a "friend" from church about what was going on that Kelley and I were publicly exposed.

Let's say we'd done a really great job of building a church of influential people from politics, media outlets, and activist organizations dedicated to social change. Which is why, when the scandal started to spread amongst the congregation, we were on the front pages of prominent newspapers and websites.

The amount of notifications my social media accounts got within hours of the scandal broke my phone. Like, actually broke it. It stopped working. My social presence I'd spent years coveting and cultivating became a nightmare of comments that no one should ever have to read about themselves.

I became the poster-boy for Christian hypocrisy. Every sermon I'd ever given was combed through to find "gotcha" quotes to take out of context. Church volunteers lined up to give interviews about my diva-like anger issues. Women from the congregation I had never even spoken to said that I had either tried and failed or successfully seduced them too. Kelley was approached by every media outlet to give an interview about how I used my power and authority to take advantage of her.

She remained silent.

The church planting organization that had helped us launch our church, gave us the funding in the early days to keep us afloat, and was our governing body, called me in to fire me.

No grace.

All truth.

Kelley stopped responding to my texts, my DMs, and my emails. She cut off all communication.

I lost everything.

If only the painful trip down memory lane could've ended there, but the flashes of memories of what happened next came fiercely.

Flashes of going home that day and screaming as I slammed the door and watching as my scared little girl ran to her room and slammed her door too.

Flashes of my wife being too depressed to get out of bed for weeks while I drank until I passed out every night.

Flashes of the news trucks in front of our house waiting

for a comment, a slip up, anything they could use for more ratings.

The final lingering memory hit me next and I could see past-me, chasing his past-wife through the house as she slammed and locked the door to our bedroom. My past-wife was protecting our past-daughter from past-me . . . I . . . kept crashing into the door until it broke open and pinned my wife down on the bed and yelled in her face, "You can't keep my daughter from me!"

I can see the fear in my past-wife and past-daughter's faces and in past-me realizing what he had become. He crumbled and slunk off the bed to the floor crying. He wiped his tears, stood up, and walked out of the house.

That's how I left.

It was the last time I saw them before I ended up in the whale.

After that, I drove drunk to a nearby parking lot where I slept for the night. The next morning, I drove to see my mom and step-dad and told them what happened. My step-dad called a guy he knew from Alcoholics Anonymous, and that's when Joal picked me up for my first meeting.

Months later, there I was . . . in a whale . . . heading to Miami Beach, where God wanted me to tell people He will, "cleanse our world with fire in forty days."

He could've picked a better man and He should've picked a better man. But He picked me.

So, why was I in the whale?

It was because of me.

I wanted to blame everyone else.

If only my parents had stayed together.

If only my wife would've said no to starting the church.

If only she wouldn't have stayed home to raise our daughter.

If only we wouldn't have hired Kelley.

If only she didn't answer the door, or let me in, or . . .

If only . . .

If only . . . I had made wise decisions.

It was me.

See what happens when you're stuck with no distractions and God has your undivided attention?

It sucks . . . until it doesn't.

I'd spent so long reacting to life and doing what I thought would make me happy. But it didn't.

I'd been doing things my own way for so long and it wasn't getting me what I wanted, so in the whale I thought, *How about I do it God's way and see what happens?*

So, I said aloud, "God, forgive me for running from You. If You want me to say what You want me to say where You want me to say it, I'm in, I'll do it. Even if it costs me whatever I have left, I trust You."

God didn't say anything.

Instead . . .

All of a sudden, the whale stuck its tongue against the roof of its mouth and smushed me in place. I couldn't move or breathe. I was very scared. I could hear the whale's heart beat quicker as we picked up a lot of speed and then . . . came to an abrupt stop.

The whale's heartbeat slowed. The tongue relaxed and I could move and breathe again. A small amount of light pierced into the mouth. It was the first light I'd seen since I had jumped off the bridge in Baltimore.

It was blinding.

I was so disoriented as the whale's mouth fell open and I birthed out onto the beach.

Right before we arrived, a man on the beach had been taking photos and videos of his kids playing in the water, and he is the one that took the video of me coming out of the whale—covered in spit, exhausted, and disoriented.

In his video, I stumble and say, "I have a message from God," as I collapse.

Who would've known this guy was a successful podcaster with hundreds of thousands of social media followers?

He didn't hesitate to upload the video to YouTube and post it for everyone to see.

The fire was lit.

CHAPTER FOUR: TWELVE WORDS AND FORTY DAYS

Day One of Forty

So that's how I ended up in the whale.

I know, I know. I could've driven myself to Miami Beach, but no . . . I had to take the hard way.

Thanks to everyone who took videos of our arrival that morning, you may know what happened next. I passed out. Help was called. People crowded around me as I was given an IV and candy bars on the tailgate of a lifeguard's truck.

It's a struggle for me to clearly remember everything that happened on the beach that morning. I was disoriented and so overwhelmed. Personally, I haven't watched many of the videos. They're all kinds of awkward for me.

I'm thankful to whoever found my backpack by the whale and brought it to me. You are a lifesaver and were clearly a part of God's plan. Much appreciated.

A local news reporter covering a different story, heard about a man spit out of a whale with a message from God, and quickly found us. He pointed a camera at my face and asked, "Who are you?"

"Eddie. Eddie White."

"Where did you come from and how'd you end up in the whale?"

I looked away as I ate the last bite of my candy bar and slowly chewed, stalling, hoping to avoid answering his questions.

"We hear you have a message from God for us, Eddie?"

Everyone held up their cameras, staring at me, waiting for me to say something. Anything.

I sat there, quietly, remembering I promised God I would do what He wanted, where He wanted me to do it. But then, surrounded by all those strangers holding their cameras in my face; the only thing I wanted to do was run.

So, I blurted out, "God is going to cleanse the world with fire in forty days."

Nailed it!

One sentence.

Twelve words.

Those twelve words launched thousands of memes, podcast episodes, sermons, hot-takes, hit-pieces, divisive political rhetoric, videos of people ranting from the driver's seat of their cars, and two professionally produced in-depth docu-series.

Speaking of memes, have you seen the one that is a still image of me—covered in whale spit, clearly looking insane —that says, in big bold white letters (outlined in black), at the top, "I HAVE A MESSAGE FROM GOD," and on the bottom, "SIR, THIS IS A WENDY'S"?

I laughed so hard the first time I saw that one. It's my favorite. Whale done.

No one has ever known till now that I actually messed up the exact wording God told me to say. I said "the world" instead of "our world" and I've wondered relentlessly over the years if it would've made a difference in what happened next or not.

To clarify, the message should've been, "God is going to cleanse OUR world with fire in forty days."

I had one job.

As soon as I said those twelve words, I got to witness what I'd like to call the worst game of telephone in the history of the world. The crowd immediately began to murmur. I could only pick up bits and pieces of conversations, different accents, and languages as they began to process what they'd heard. A few people started crying, a lot looked shocked, but most of them seemed confused. I can imagine everyone was hoping for the Good News but, instead, they got the Bad News.

Really, really, *really* Bad News.

The tiny flames were being fanned.

You know in the Bible when Jesus said something that upset the crowd and they wanted to stone Him, but somehow, He slipped through to safety . . . I did that! Look, I'm no Jesus, but I get now how He did it. Everyone was so concerned about themselves that they didn't even notice Him walk right through. That's exactly how I did it.

As I put distance between myself and the crowd and the whale, I looked back, and saw a man run wildly into the surf. It looked like he was trying to baptize himself under the waves. He must've received the message loud and clear and was choosing to do something about it.

Since my "heavenly work" was finished, I wanted to get the whale spit off me and change my clothes; because although I couldn't smell myself, I imagined I smelled like a thousand rotting fish. I crossed over the wooden boardwalk that separates the beaches from the parking lots and hotels and suddenly realized where the whale had beached us. It was the same hotel, on exactly the one-year anniversary, where I had broken my vows and been unfaithful to my wife, with Kelley.

Subtle God, real subtle. He literally brought me back to the place I'd been metaphorically running from. It's the main reason I didn't want to go back to Miami Beach. I never wanted to see that beach or hotel again.

As I entered the hotel lobby, it looked and smelled exactly the same as before, and I saw the ghosts of past-me and past-Kelley everywhere. I quickly walked past the receptionist, past the bar, past the breakfast nook, all the way outside, to the pool. I snagged a used towel from the return bin and took a much-needed refreshing outdoor shower. I washed all the spit off before heading to the poolside bathroom to change into the gym clothes I had with me in my backpack.

Thank goodness for my backpack.

My backpack is waterproof and submersible and I still use it all the time. I got it as a Father's Day gift from my wife. I asked for one because I loved walking and scooting to work, even on rainy days, and I wanted something to keep my books and things dry. We rented a similar one before when we went hiking through a river at a National Park. When I first got it, I had no idea how beneficial it would be to my future-self.

This is my online review for the backpack:

"5/5 . . . would buy again. Works as advertised, even inside a whale's mouth. Highly recommend!"

Once I was in the bathroom, I finally saw what happened to my hair. It seems that an enzyme in the whale's saliva stripped all the color from my beard, eyebrows, and everything else. My hair is now a stark white and no matter how much I've tried to dye it, nothing's ever worked to change it.

God marked me with a constant reminder of my time in the whale.

I'm thankful I didn't know about the "whitening" before the crowd on the beach recorded all those videos and took lots of pictures of me. I might have been self-conscious about it.

I changed into my wrinkled and musty gym clothes as I kept staring at my white hair in the mirror. Then it all hit me . . . I finally realized, God said through me, that He was going to cleanse our world with fire in forty days. I hadn't really thought about the content of His message and what it meant until then. I was so consumed with being mute, my life burning down, finding the fox in the hen house, running from hoards of homeless people, getting swallowed by a whale, spit out on the beach, all those cameras in my face, that I hadn't thought about what God told me to say.

OMG!

I wanted to get home to my family.

I needed a car.

I knew of a church not far from the hotel—that I and our church had supported in the past. They were the main reason we chose to visit Miami Beach for our off-site team-building trip the year before. The church was close enough to hike to and I hoped my old friend, Miguel, the pastor, would help me if I asked.

I was about to leave the hotel, when I felt the Holy Spirit nudge me to visit the room I had stayed in the year before. I considered ignoring the feeling, but I realized it was one of those opportunities to start following God's Will instead of my own.

I took the stairs to the second floor, to room 205. I stood outside the room and thought about everything that had happened inside. I put my hand on the door and prayed, "Lord, I am sorry for the decisions I made in this room. Please forgive me. Amen."

Then I felt another nudge to retrace my steps, from my room to Kelley's. Her room had been on the seventh floor, room 719. I remembered how my body trembled as I walked down the hallway, pushed the elevator button, and waited till one arrived, how I entered it, hit the button for the seventh floor, stopped a few times to let others off on their floors, and then walked down the hallway to her room.

So many opportunities to stop and go back.

I could see the ghost of past-me pacing back and forth outside the room. I put my hand on the door and prayed, "God, help me make amends for what happened here. Please. Amen."

There was something restorative about going back to where I had made unwise decisions. There wasn't an immediate change, but it did feel like I was taking the literal steps of repentance.

Little did I know I would have so much more to repent for in the following days.

When I got to the church, it was overwhelmed by a large crowd outside, looking for answers. Miguel was standing on the roof of a car in the parking lot, fielding questions, and giving an impromptu sermon on salvation, repentance, and baptism.

Miguel and I met at a church planting conference, about a year after our church in D.C. launched. I was there as a guest for a panel discussion on church life during the first year. He introduced himself after the panel and asked if I would consider mentoring him. Even though I was Miguel's mentor, it always felt like he was mentoring me, through his example, on faith and spiritual disciplines.

I helped him launch his first Sunday service and now I needed his help.

It looked like the church staff and volunteers were hurrying to set up an inflatable kiddie pool so they could baptize new converts. God's Message had spread quickly. I kept a low profile and asked a volunteer to find Miguel and let him know an old friend from D.C. needed to talk with him. It took about twenty minutes of waiting, but Miguel finally found me. When he realized it was me, he dropped to his knees in reverence.

Wasn't expecting that.

I quickly told him to stand up, because he was freaking me

out. We talked for a few minutes about the whale and the forty days and then I asked for his car so I could get home to my family. He reached into his pocket, gave me the key, and pointed to his car in the parking lot. It was not a great car. But it was a car and I was grateful. He asked if I needed money or anything else. I told him gas money would be great. He handed me all the money he had in his wallet; it was about thirty-five dollars.

He said, "It's the least I can do for God's prophet."

Wasn't expecting that either.

Thank God for Miguel. I really appreciated what he did for me that day. I still feel bad that I never returned his car to him. I did make it up to him . . . eventually.

The road trip home was lonely. I missed the *dum dum, dum dum, dum dum* of the whale's heart. The whale and the car had two things in common: how cramped and how hot they were. Miguel's car didn't have air conditioning. Who lives in South Florida in the middle of the summer and doesn't have air conditioning? I was thankful for the car, but wow, it was hot.

I drove the whole way home with the windows down.

Fortunately, the radio worked and I turned it up loud enough to hear it over the noise of the wind. It didn't take long before I heard a radio DJ mention the whale and me. "Looks like a disgraced former pastor of a church in D.C., who was fired because of a sex scandal, got spit out by a whale in Miami Beach today."

That hurt.

"The Whale Man said he had a message from God, something about the world being destroyed in forty days."

It was the first time I heard someone call me the Whale Man.

"Looks like we'll all be planning end-of-the-world parties now," he said as he turned on REM's "It's the End of the World as We Know It."

It wasn't the response I expected.

Soon after, I made a pit stop for gas about two hundred miles north from Miguel's church. I went inside the store to use the bathroom and when I came out the car was surrounded by strangers. They must have spotted me while I was pumping gas. I really didn't think anyone would recognize me. At first, I thought the crowd might attack me but, instead, a woman showed me a child in her arms and asked, "Can you please heal my daughter?"

I wasn't prepared for that.

"I don't think that's a thing I can do," I said, instead of asking what was wrong. I've spent the last couple of years wondering if God would have healed her through me if I had believed that I could. I replay that day in my head and I imagine putting my hand on the child's head and praying for God to heal her, and miraculously He does.

I regret not trying.

A man from the crowd reached out and grabbed my forearm and asked, "Are you the Whale Man?" It startled me and I almost punched him. He immediately fell to the ground, convulsed, and spoke in tongues . . . loudly. Surprisingly, the crowd completely ignored him.

Someone yelled out, "Is Jesus coming back?" And another asked, "What can we do to make God change his mind?"

I didn't feel equipped to help these people and they were

preventing me from going home. So, I asked everyone to take a knee so I could pray for them. I prayed out loud, "God, please hear the questions and pleas from these people. Help them find the answers they are looking for, as they let me drive away, so I can continue to do Your Will."

Subtle.

It worked and they parted like the Red Sea as I got back into the car. The woman with the sick young child in her arms yelled out, "God bless you Whale Man," as I drove away. It's the strangest sentence anyone has ever said to me.

I did think about their questions as I drove home.

Was Jesus coming back in forty days?

Maybe.

Could we do something to change God's mind?

Hopefully.

I spent the rest of the road trip keeping a low profile whenever I needed to stop. It was a long and lonely trip home. The wind and the radio kept me company. Although the radio was a constant reminder of how much I really disliked the world. Flipping from station to station, there were a lot of jokes, commentary, and debate about me, the whale, and God's message.

It was a blessing I didn't have a working phone with me. Months later, when I finally looked at what happened to my social media accounts and how many posts and tweets I was tagged in, with everything from death threats to marriage proposals, it was overwhelming.

I missed the quiet of the whale.

It was in North Carolina that I realized I hadn't taken a

meditation break since the whale spit me out. I pulled over at a rest area and did my normal ten-minute routine, but... woke up a few hours later. I didn't want to sleep, but I guess that's exactly what my body needed. I'd been running off adrenaline and energy drinks since I left Miami. I hadn't eaten much since the chicken I ordered from Fox at the Hen House Chicken and Fish. Thinking about the chicken made me wonder how that kid was doing and if he ever knew he'd been a part of God's plan for me.

On the road again, I heard numerous news reports about the massive pilgrimage of believers and skeptics gathering near the site of the whale on the beach. The authorities tried to shut down the beach, but people overran their barricades. They wanted to either touch God's whale or at least get a selfie with it.

#whalelife was trending.

And so was #whereisthewhaleman.

It took a couple more hours on the road to finally get home, and that's when my worst nightmare came true. It was invaded by news trucks and what looked like a mob of people searching for answers. The whole way home, I hadn't thought about people finding out where I lived.

Apparently, when I gave my name to the reporter on the beach, the world descended on my house and began knocking on my front door. My wife had been dropping our daughter off at school that morning and when she got back to the house, it was surrounded.

She'd lived through news crews on our lawn before, when the scandal with Kelley broke, but this time she didn't know why they were there. She told me that she was afraid something bad happened to me, since I'd missed story time with our daughter the night before and wasn't responding to her texts.

As she got out of the car, a reporter asked her what she thought about what happened in Miami. She was confused and said she didn't know and asked what happened. The reporter said, "Your husband was spat out of a whale on Miami Beach this morning with a message from God. He said that God is going to destroy the world with fire in forty days. Do you know where he is?"

Imagine her surprise.

When I pictured my homecoming, it didn't look like this. I don't know what I thought would happen when I made it home. I left on the worst of terms and we hadn't addressed any of our issues since I'd been gone. I do know, this wasn't the way I wanted to return.

What if they don't want me home?

What if someone tries to hurt me?

What if I make everything worse?

My "what ifs of fear" thoughts came fast.

I'd given a popular sermon years before about the "what ifs of fear" and the "what ifs of hope" thoughts we have. The "what ifs of fear" keep us from becoming who God has made us to be. The "what ifs of hope" help us to become who God has made us to be. The kind of "what ifs" thoughts we choose to listen to and follow, over time, will become the loudest we hear and will eventually drown out the other.

That day, my "what ifs of fear" thoughts won.

I drove away . . . to a nearby 24-hour Walmart to contemplate my lack of options. If only I'd taken the time to meditate so I could've cleared my mind and seriously thought about my next right steps. I wasn't thinking, I was only reacting to my feelings. And I felt the best thing to do was to run away again.

Yes, I too can see a pattern in my behavior.

Inside Walmart, I purchased a small tent, food and water, flashlights and a head lamp, sleeping bag, portable radio, batteries, toilet paper, and new clothes. I used the self-checkout so I didn't have to talk with anyone. Before I left, I cashed out all the money I could for the day from the ATM.

My plan was to hide out in the woods at a nearby state park that my wife and I had hiked through many times. I knew of areas off-trail that I could set up a small tent and live off the grid for a couple of days, until the media moved onto the next story. I learned from my last experience with them that they'd quickly move find something better.

Unfortunately, the mystery of where I was is what kept the story alive. Plus, the fascination of the whale. Oh . . . and the countdown to God's fiery biblical cleansing. I clearly underestimated how much of a good news story this all was.

Heavy sigh.

Before I got to the trailhead at the park, I found a pay phone (a pay phone?) and called my wife. She didn't answer. When I eventually asked her about it, she said she'd been getting so many calls from unknown numbers that she'd sent everything to voicemail, but she'd been hoping for me to call.

I left her this voicemail, "Hey, it's me, I'm safe and I love you. I want to come home. Everything is so messed up. I don't want to tell you where I am right now, because I don't want anyone to know. It's safer that way. I'm sorry . . . for everything. You deserved and deserve better. Please tell our sweet little girl that I'll do story time soon and that I love and miss her so much." I was crying as I hung up the phone.

She saved it.

The sun was starting to come up as I left the trail and found a flat spot to set up camp. I put the radio I bought underneath the sleeping bag, by my head, like a pillow. I put my ear on the speaker so only I could hear it. I fell asleep listening to the news. It was cold that morning. I missed the warmth of the whale and the *dum dum, dum dum, dum dum.*

One day alone in the woods turned into many more.

Day Seventeen (I think) of Forty

My "what ifs of fear" kept me isolated in the woods. I starved for a few days before I discovered the joys of nighttime dumpster diving at a sports pub close enough for me to hike to. I could've bought food with the money I had with me, but I was too afraid to be seen.

I quickly learned the holy grail of dumpster diving is the to-go boxes people forget to take home with them. You can find burgers, baked potatoes, and lots of cold french fries. I skipped salads, desserts, and anything with dairy in it. This place made the best homemade brownies. Finding one of those in a to-go box was like finding buried treasure. I did have to scrape off the ice cream.

If you ever wondered where I was during the Forty Days, I was dumpster diving for sweet, sweet brownies.

During the nights, I dumpster dove (dived?), and during the

days, I listened to AM talk-radio so I could hear what was happening in the world.

The world was metaphorically and literally on fire.

Conflicts broke out in the Middle East and elsewhere.

Religious zealots set fires everywhere, "helping" God with the cleansing process.

Churches, synagogues, and mosques, around the world, were full whenever their doors were open.

But, for most people, nothing changed for them. They didn't believe in God before the whale and they didn't believe in Him after the whale. They lived their lives like they always had. I envied their ignorance.

The loneliness of the woods was fertile soil for my seeds of despair. My internal chatterbox of negative self-talk got stuck on repeat. My "what ifs of fear" became louder and louder with each passing day until they were the only "what ifs" I could hear.

I kept digging a hole too deep to climb out of.

It was around this time, I think it was Day Seventeen, that I approached the sports pub dumpster; and hidden behind it were six bottles of good bourbon in an unopened box. My guess is that a worker stashed them out there on a trash run and was planning to take them home at the end of their shift. I'd love to say I started pacing when I saw them and recited the Serenity Prayer and was strong enough to leave them there. But, that's not what happened.

I snatched them.

I forgot all about finding those sweet, sweet brownies in the dumpster and took the whole box back to my campsite and got drunk and then yelled at God. I don't recall exactly what I yelled, but here is the gist of my ranting:

"I did what You asked me to do and now I'm here all alone and everyone hates me. You did this to me. You didn't give me a choice. You caused everyone to hate me. I hate You! I hate the life You've given me. Why didn't You let me drown? I wish You would've picked someone else. If this is what it's like to love You, then I don't want it. Go love someone else."

I eventually passed out—pissed off, sad, and hoping to never wake up.

But, I did.

So, I got drunk again, yelled at God again, and passed out again—pissed off, sad, and hoping to never wake up.

And again the next day.

And the next.

And when I ran out of the "free" bourbon I found, I walked to a liquor store near the park and bought more. No one recognized me. The clerks behind the counter never relayed any new demands from God. It was as if God had used me and forgotten all about me.

Alone, drunk, and angry is how I spent the rest of the Forty Days.

My fire was raging.

#thisiswherethewhalemanwas

CHAPTER FIVE: SO MUCH GRACE

I missed so much while I was alone in the woods for those Forty Days.

The batteries in my radio died around Day Thirty-Two, so I missed the hurricane that struck Miami on the morning of Day Forty. The storm surge swept away what was left of the whale and the shrines and any evidence we'd ever been there.

I missed the global cease-fire on Day Thirty-Eight when all the conflicts in the world stopped . . . for a few days.

I missed the Night of Prayer on Day Thirty-Nine, when religions of the world came together to ask God to relent.

Looks like it worked.

Well done, everyone.

There was no rapture or fiery biblical destruction of the earth.

Life kept going.

My life kept going.

I was relieved and . . . a little disappointed.

By Day Forty-Three, my rage toward God had faded into

apathy. I was more upset about the sports pub locking their dumpster at night than I was about the world believing I was a false prophet.

I was starving, thirsty, and tired of being isolated, so I left the woods and went to a nearby convenience store where I'd spent the rest of my money on water and food, since I no longer had a dumpster in which to dive. I sat down in front of it and asked the strangers that passed by for change, so I could eat.

That was my official Day One of being without a home.

Initially, I was worried people would recognize me, but no one ever did. They barely looked at me. Most people either kept their distance so they wouldn't have to engage with me or quickly glanced as they said, "God bless," and dropped change in my cup.

To everyone who blessed me with money, dropped off a bottle of water, or handed me food: you sustained me and I'm grateful.

Thank you.

Yes, I did buy alcohol with your money, and, yes, I did pass out from time to time on the sidewalk. And I did get yelled at by a few people to "get a job." But, thankfully, not another homeless person ever shouted at me, "You can't run from God, Eddie," and that . . . that was a blessing.

Over time, I got to know others on the streets, like my friend Marcus. He's a slender and rugged looking gentleman in his early-fifties. Marcus thinks we're the same height, but we checked and I'm a little taller than him. He'd been living on the streets for a few years. We'd sit for hours swapping stories and he helped me with tips for surviving on my own.

After we spent a few days getting to know each other, I asked Marcus, "So what happened?" He got quiet for a moment and he told me, "I caught my wife and my best friend together in my own bed." He told me that he hasn't been able to trust anyone ever since. He lost his job, got behind on bills, and ended up living on the streets.

There was an abundance of sadness in his eyes.

I asked Marcus, "Do you think you could ever forgive them?" I was really asking for me, because I was hoping that forgiveness was possible. He said, with tears in his eyes, "I could never forgive them for what they did to me."

Talking with Marcus helped me finally realize that, deep down, the reason I hadn't gone home was because I knew that if my wife had done to me what I had done to her, I wouldn't have been able to forgive her.

I would've thrown the first stone at her.

Marcus wiped his tears and asked, "So, why are you here?" I told him that I'd made a series of unwise decisions and walked out on my family and then lived on my own for a while until God burned down my job and apartment on the same day. Then I got swallowed by a whale and it spit me out on a beach in Miami where I delivered a message from God that He was going to destroy the world in forty days. But, then He didn't, and now I was afraid to be seen because everyone hated me. Marcus looked at me with all sincerity and told me, "You gotta stay away from the drugs."

My days of living on the street blurred together.

One day I was panhandling, when, all of a sudden, across the street from me, a street preacher set up his mobile church. He was wearing a full-length homemade sign, THE END IS NEAR, and preaching very loudly.

Sigh.

I listened to him rant about Hell and salvation and repentance and then I was shocked as he said, "THE WHALE MAN HAS COMETH! HE WAS OUR WARNING! A LIGHTHOUSE IN THE SEA! GOD HAS GIVEN US TIME TO REPENT AND GIVE UP OUR LIVES OF SIN BEFORE IT IS TOO LATE! FIRE IS STILL COMING!"

It was nice to get a shoutout.

Maybe street preachers weren't so bad after all.

I was building a new life for myself. I'd developed a good daily routine. I found safe places to spend the nights. I made new friends and all my needs were being met. At night, a lot of us would meet up at a covered bus stop to sleep. We'd tell jokes and stories until we passed out for the night.

Life was ok.

One morning, I woke up late and everyone else had already gone; I noticed a flier had been left by my head. It was for a local shelter and it mentioned hot showers and hot meals. I couldn't remember the last time I'd had a hot shower or a full plate of food, so I used the map on the flier to hike straight there.

I was greeted by a kind volunteer that showed me to the showers and told me I could take any of the donated clean clothes I wanted. The shower was glorious. It was the kind where you stand there and watch the dirt run off your body and down the drain. After taking the longest shower of my life, I shaved off my white beard and styled my white hair for the first time since Miami.

The hot shower, fresh shave, and clean clothes made me feel like a new man.

Now, it was time to eat.

I immediately noticed this radiant female volunteer at the end of the food line. I wasn't attracted to her; she reminded me of my wife when she was younger and what I imagined our daughter might look like when she gets older. I tried not to stare as I made my way down to her.

When I got to her station, she smiled at me and scooped a big pile of french fries onto my plate. She kept trying to make eye contact, but I looked away. I was worried she'd recognize who I was since I'd shaven.

I looked around at all the tables and found a place to sit by myself.

As soon as I began to eat, the radiant volunteer walked straight toward me. I noticed she had a lanyard with the name "ROOT" written on it. She stood in front of me and asked, "May I sit with you, Eddie?"

Busted.

In my head I yelled, *No no no no!*

I kept looking at my food, eating, hoping she'd go away.

She sat down without me answering and asked, "How are you doing Eddie?" I continued to ignore her because I was worried that she was a reporter and that the whole place was about to be swarmed with news crews. Instead, she said, "Don't worry Eddie, I'm not a reporter and this place isn't about to be swarmed with news crews."

It was like she was in my head.

"Why are you here, Eddie?"

"I think you have me confused with someone else, my name's not Eddie."

"You're right, your real name is Edgar Jacob White. You told people to call you Eddie in the sixth grade because you thought it sounded cooler."

I was stunned, and she used that opportunity to snag a fry from my plate.

Rude.

"Who are you?" I asked as I sheltered my food with one hand.

She reached across the table to shake the other.

"I am Lauren."

I glanced around at the others in the room and then shook her hand and quietly said, "I am Whale Man."

She smiled.

"Why are you here, Edgar?"

"Things didn't work out the way I planned."

She snagged another fry as I let my guard down.

Annoyed.

I asked, "Why are you here, Lauren?"

"I'm here for you, Edgar. I've been waiting for you so I could talk with you."

Confused.

She asked, "Why are you here when you have family and friends that love you and want you to come home?"

Defeated.

"No, they don't. I messed everything up. They're better off without me."

Lauren held out her hand again and asked, "Edgar, would you please hand me the Bible in your backpack?"

"How do you know I have that in my backpack?"

She didn't respond. She kept waiting for me to hand it to her.

I took the Bible out of my backpack and handed it to her and she began flipping through the pages. She found the Step Nine list I had tucked in there and placed it on the table next to her. I hadn't looked at that list since I stuck it in there the night before my apartment burned down. When I glanced at the names, I realized there was more to make amends for now.

Heavy sigh.

"These handwritten messages are beautiful. It looks like a lot of people love you and your wife."

"Loved," I said as I watched her.

She read one of the messages out loud, "Thank you both for being so kind and for teaching me that God loves me and cares about me, even when I can't see it."

Her voice reminded me of my favorite elementary school teacher who read us stories as we sat crisscross applesauce on the circle carpet.

My eyes got misty.

She flipped through a few more pages and read another one, "You taught me about God's love and grace and I appreciate you both so much."

She was about to read another, when I said, "Stop . . . please."

Lauren pulled a pen from her pocket and said, "I'm going to write something too." She searched and found a specific page and began to write. Then she took the Step Nine list and wrote on it, too, and then tucked it back into the Bible, like a bookmark for that page.

She handed everything back to me and gestured that it was ok for me to read it.

I turned to the page she'd bookmarked and read what she'd written and where she'd written it. Tears began to stream from my eyes. Like, serious tears. Like the kind that start to flow and then it's all kinds of ugly crying.

I still tear up when I think of this moment.

If you're wondering what she wrote and where she wrote it . . . I'll tell you at the end.

But, I can tell you right now that it changed me.

As I composed myself, I asked her again, "Who are you?"

"I am Lauren," she said confidently as she leaned in to whisper, "What if they're not mad? What if they're not waiting to judge you for where you've been and what you've done? What if they want you to come home?"

I started trembling.

"It's time."

"It's time to go home, Edgar," she said as she stood up and walked away for forever.

I sat there.

For a while.

I came up with a comprehensive plan to clean myself up, get a job, find a place to live, and become worthy of my wife and daughter again. Then I'd go to them and ask for their forgiveness and hope they'd allow me to be a part of their lives again.

It felt like a good plan and I was motivated to get started. But, as I walked out the door of the shelter, I saw something I never expected to see, it was a missing poster with my photo on it.

EDGAR WHITE.

MISSING SINCE JULY 31.

WE LOVE YOU AND MISS YOU!

PLEASE COME HOME!

The poster had hand drawn hearts on it that I knew my daughter had done.

Ugly crying.

Again.

When I looked around, I saw missing posters all over the place. It looked like they'd been there for a few days. I hadn't noticed them on my way to the shelter. I must've been looking at the ground the whole time.

New plan.

I immediately started hiking the eight miles home. The half-day journey gave me time to mentally prepare to knock on the door to our home. Every time a "what if of fear" came to mind, I forced it into a "what if of hope."

What if they don't welcome me home? became, *What if they do welcome me home?*

About a mile from our house, I stopped at an empty neighborhood playground, and took a ten-minute meditation break. I was excited and anxious and wanted my thoughts to be clear as I walked up to the front door. During those ten minutes, I felt the Holy Spirit nudging me to make a list of "what ifs of hope" for the future.

On the back of the Step Nine list I wrote:

What if we laugh and love again?

What if we share life and joy again?

What if we are enough?

I felt ready for what came next. Well, kind of. I was still trembling and wanted to throw up a little.

When I got to our street, I could see a bunch of cars parked in front of our home, but, thankfully, no news trucks. I kept expecting to get ambushed. As I approached the driveway, I saw someone had spray painted "FALSE PROPHET" on the front of the house.

At least they'd spelled prophet correctly.

I knocked on the front door and braced for impact. One of our original youth group kids, Andrew, who helped us launch the church, answered the door. He instantly recognized me and yelled out to a house full of search volunteers, friends, and family, "EDDIE'S HOME!"

My daughter burst through the house screaming, "DADDY!" She pushed past everyone and threw her arms around my waist and squeezed me tight. She'd gotten so big since the last time I saw her. I picked her up and held her close.

"Did you see our signs?!"

"I did baby girl."

"Did you see the hearts I drew on them?"

"I did."

"Did you like them?"

"I loved them."

"Where were you?"

"I got lost."

"Did you get unlost?"

"Yes."

"Where's your whale, daddy?"

"The whale is gone, sweetheart."

"I missed story time."

"I have so many new stories for you."

"Yay!"

I had my eyes closed soaking in the moment and when I opened them my wife was standing right in front of us.

Her eyes were misty and she was smiling.

She wrapped her arms around us both and kissed me on my face and whispered gently in my ear, "Welcome home."

We both let out the longest sighs.

I whispered back, "I'm so sorry."

"Shh, I know, we can talk about it tomorrow."

"I love you."

"I love you."

EPILOGUE: NO STONES

The next day we began the difficult and redemptive work of restoration and reconciliation.

My updated STEP NINE list:

- my wife ✓
- my daughter ✓
- Kelley ✓
- the church ✓
- the world
- ~~God~~ GRACE ✓

Lauren had crossed out "God" on my list and replaced it with GRACE ✓.

That was after she found John 8:11 in my Bible, circled it with her red pen, and wrote these words, just like this, in the margin:

So

A

Beautiful

Story

Of

Redemption

And

Love

Could

Be

Told

Made in the USA
Monee, IL
14 June 2022

97998713R00049